RANDOM MUSINGS OF A TECHIE

ROY PADMANABHAN

ISBN 979-888591723-0

Deepthy

Deva and Nandu

Contents

ACKNOWLEDGEMENTS

This short collection would never be possible without the love from my wife Deepthy and our kids Deva and Nandu. They were always my very first readers and true sources of inspiration to appreciate the little things in life. And a big thanks to my amazing circle of friends for their comments, thoughts and constant encouragement to write. Most importantly, thanks to the wonderful people I met along the way that come in as characters here.

I

The Little Things That Matter

This might feel a little odd, but true. How come one regret missing a 7:30PM show of Grand Old Mumbai circus, even after a long 20 years? Reactions vary from ridiculous, to outrageous to simply a non-issue. But this turns out to be a little more sensitive issue than you can imagine. Parashuraman a.k.a Pash is my ex-colleague. Having spent years together in a venerable Govt. of India Research Lab in the earlier stages of our career, we parted ways but were destined to meet again to travel together on yet another roller coaster. Over a lager late last evening, Pash recollected the circus incident.

Grand old Mumbai circus had just landed in Trivandrum. Posters sprouted all along the Kowdiar stretch, Palayam and Statue area. The unblemished Russian teens demonstrating their uncanny abilities in the ring, the jokers sporting the mundane, yet refreshing, costumes, the old yet majestic tuskers, and the king of the jungle sans its aggression. Pash was so excited that our bike rides along the Kowdiar stretch to the office in the morning rush hours were unusually longer.

Later one evening, Pash flipped open his wallet and showed off a green Rs.50 first class pass. He was planning to watch the 7:30PM show over the weekend. Being part of the same team working on a key strategic project of the organization, I was not sure about making it over the weekend, especially when the first prototype was up for a scheduled testing. But Pash was confident of sailing it through and pack off well before 4PM that evening. The visiting officer from the collaborating firm was keen to get the testing done on day one itself. Everything was going pretty well, until we noticed a problem with the power supply. This was causing unsolicited signals in the input gate and the system started malfunctioning. Pash was cool handling it until he noticed the hour needle closing on to 7PM. Shutting down the unit, he put on his watch, packed his bag, and started to leave. The gentle man frowned and shouted. Pash explained the reason why he should leave. Brazen, to say the least, was my take on it! How could you ever think of watching a circus when a priority work in office was still pending? "Let me speak to your boss, I need to understand the priority of this work", the gentleman continued to be aggressive on getting the stuff done. Half an hour later, Pash was back at work, pulled out his Rs.50 pass and tore it off in the trash. I smiled inside, you need to have your wisdom to choose priorities mate.

But now, stepping into Pash's shoe, watching a circus that has been in your list of to do things for long was a must do. Life is not all about work, earning and spending. It is also about the little things that we cherish, that we are so passionate about, that peps us up. Reading through your favorite book, sipping coffee in a cold windy evening, walking along the beach holding hands with your loved ones, watching your kids play hide and seek, the early morning workouts that you have been planning so long, drinking wine in the company of your partner, and talking through the wee hours, enjoying that fiesta siesta combo on a lazy Saturday afternoon. Watching your little ones on stage on school day, attending their first dance performance, cooking your favorite dish with your partner, gossiping, and talking through the day's rigors. The list could be endless.

All these matter, and they don't pass onto the trivia list. But my early twenties were too early to figure this out. But yes, I didn't have the luxury of so many gray cells then!

On a side real note: prototypes seldom work.

II

The Moves

I have always been a little paranoid when it comes to moves; didn't quite look up the dictionary yet to see if there is an established definition for that phobia, but the mere feeling and experience beats the literary definition hands down.

The workplace move was relatively easy, though bidding farewell to the tranquil beach city of Long Beach was apparently painful. My fourth-floor office opened straight up to the runway of the LGB airport, offering unhindered views of the planes gliding in and taking off every now and then. Driving back home from the last day of work there, the back seats of my car were loaded with the little belongings that decked up the soft boards and the desk. A pin up of the family enjoying a beach holiday, kids' graduation pictures, a few pencil sketches by the elder one, and a handwritten Father's Day note from the younger one were the picks of the lot. A dog-eared copy of the *Monk who sold his Ferrari* and the *Chicken soup for the dad's soul* had moved with me several times over the last ten years.

The runway facing workplace gave way to an urban cubicle, with the plethora of animation movie characters bringing cheers to my days. My personal paraphernalia found yet another new home waiting for the next move.

And hardly two months after, here we go setting up home again. The unopened boxes of household items are still lining up the living room. The paintings and the family pictures are still waiting for their semi-permanent spots on the wall. The curios know they will surely return to their prominent spots, but now it's time to be patient. The wine rack and my precious age-old collections lie elsewhere. Stacks of birthday cards from the kids and wife line up beneath the loads of books and unopened envelopes.

Up ahead in the distance, I see the Hollywood hills, lighting up the darkness engulfing the city. Got to go back to bed with the excitement of setting up home again, an inevitable part of a transient's life.

III

Two-bedroom Mansions!

Is there really a thing called a two-bedroom mansion? Arguably, yes. But then, there are plethora of reasons to throw a skeptic in dismay, especially when one lives a stone's throw away from the insanely upscale communities in Hollywood and the Beverly Hills! Rather, the questions tend to veer off slightly and take the forms such as: do you really get to meet the Hollywood celebrities in person? Well, kind of. On a real note, I can actually hear the Maseraties whizzing past elsewhere up north.

Let me come back to the two-bedroom mansions. They do exist, and it is a non-negotiable fact. When you sit on the couch and watch the gorgeous and charismatic Ellen DeGeneres spending an elevated funny moment with Bruno Mars, you could easily catch a glimpse of the elder teen across the corridor wrapping up her week-end project work. Lean back for a moment and give a slight wink, and there you catch up with the younger one; the newbie teen trying to rescue (read 'in vain') the whole world from evil and the invading alien monsters. He is almost there; it might take him the rest of the day to possibly wrap up that never ending fun games. The dude talks to me about all those weird serious matters ever since he lost that puppy breath and sooner, we will do that man to man talk. Diagonally across the room is our bibliophile's paradise; a five-storied wooden housing that displays Laura Ingalls to Nora Roberts, Harry Potter to John Grisham, Shashi Tharoor to RK Narayan, MK Menon to Madhavikkutty, and The College Board's NEW SAT Bible just to make that diversity perfect.

The wine cellar (six bottles at peak capacity) is right across your left, slightly above eye level on the loft. Cherishing the short sabbatical from work, my wife devours her favorite authors from the other corner in the hallway. We can always shout out to each other; for a glass of wine, talking through the day's rigors or gossiping on that ex-colleague of mine whom we equally loved to the bottom of our hearts. Talking about my cellar, it almost slipped my mind. Our mini bar is well stocked 24x7 for any pop-up guest. The JDs to Tequilas, that weird Hawaiian Rum to the Old Monk; not an endless repertoire, but pretty decent. We almost always ask the guest's preference by pointing to the label right from the couch, not missing the animated thread of conversations by a whisker.

The best part is when you are able to relieve yourself with a washroom trip in precisely three steps. Just sneak in and sneak out, period. And no baroque, winding stairs to climb up to catch up a long week-end siesta in the bedroom. Those journeys can sometimes be arduously painful and monotonous is what my friend who actually owns a mansion said.

I know my defensive story is never complete without talking about our sprawling pool. All that luxury view, plus the spa that comes as super bonus, is any waterbody's pleasure from our pool view bedroom. Take a step back and slightly pull apart those window blinds; you could enjoy our miniature garden on the railings, including a rare species of cactus from the tropicals.

Summing up, it's just a cluttered mess of happiness where we bump onto each other all the time, with frequent hugs, occasional shout outs and parental sermons. Yes, mansions do exist in two-bedroom forms; you surely got to re-do that classic definition slightly to see it. Or feel free to pop-up any time of the day for a hands-on experience.

A little guy who visited us with family was too quizzical when I told him this is our mansion. Please view this as my sincere attempt to clarify why I stand by that.

IV

The Cupcake Fridays

Jen Frazier serves cupcakes on her desk every Friday. You would feel that sweet, mild aroma of those cute little cakes when you pass the corner off the fourth-floor cafe. This workplace transforms itself on every Friday post lunch when Jen displays her little creations on her tiny desk, tucked off in the corner. Numerous post its that talk about things accomplished and those yet to be done for the upcoming week, pictures of her husband enjoying a game of golf, her girls in their proms, and pompom the pup in a pink outfit. The place could easily spread cheers around, even to a passerby on the hallway.

Fruity almonds, a layer of caramel on chocolate sponge sprinkled with finely chopped dry fruits, layers of vanilla topped with apple jelly and a dash of peanut butter; they come in varied forms, colors, and outfits. The cups come in unique designs, some hand painted, and others crafted with amazingly creative micro-origami work.

The endless array of these sweet little things gets cleared momentarily. If you are not in the first few cup aficionados, you are in for a wait, for yet another Friday. The unsolicited guests leave, thanking Jen and in anticipation of another Friday. Jen continues work, her contagious laughter spreading cheers all around in a pretty cuppy way.

Given the growing number of Jen fans in our office, someone of late has advised her to start a home-based business. I get it, a very natural and harmless thought from a well-wisher. But then, who will spread cheers around in an otherwise mundane workplace on a Friday afternoon? The cheers disappear when dollar comes in, won't they?

V

Prized Possessions

While cleaning up my son's bedroom, I bumped onto a plethora of seemingly trivia, non-sense and 'why do you need to keep these' kinda stuff. Weeding them out altogether was not in the least of my intentions this time. His cribbing and nonstop whining lasted for hours when I tossed a torn-up picture of a superhero into the dustbin during one of those cleaning missions last time. In his own verbiage, I was ruthless, mercilessly rude, and callous; to say the least. His vehemence and unflinching opinions on my incendivity made me ponder a bit, going beyond those mundane household chores.

If you see a bunny eared notebook, with half the pages torn up with those crayon arts scattered all over, that could most possibly be their travel journal. You probably did not notice the name tag and the subject written on the very first page in a wavy cursive (and sometimes in mixed print). Well, it's their journal, and that's how they document their memoirs. Way different from ours and our perceptions. And it is available right their when they have the best of creative mindset to jot down something. The bookshelf would not be a wise choice for that since you need to hunt the book down when you feel to write something. A spoil sport indeed!

A long-folded piece of double ruled notebook sheets, with red pointy edges could well be their weaponry. You will mostly fail to notice the faded-out letters on the sides, saying 'World War II re-enacted'. Again, stay off and be safe. Art rules in those little minds.

A semi-dried leaf, with a wooden piece wrapped up in a butter paper could well be their prized possession from a national park. Be safe than sorry in ignoring those during your cleaning missions.

An almost used up eraser and a broken pencil sharpener under their bed could be the one their teacher presented for helping her in the Computer Class. You could probably pack off their pencil boxes with new ones from Staples, but again, stay off from those prized possessions. You cannot replace them.

The manifolded square sheet of wide ruled paper almost finds its place in the bin. But then, you notice the messy handwriting with their name and a happy birthday note just below. Their best friend's greeting card on their birthdays could not be sweeter.

A small Hershey's in a foil wrap could well be the return gift from another friend's birthday party last week.

The half-read Laura Ingalls would be under the bed; and another Wimpy Kid Diary could be under the pillow. Convenience matters, and tidiness doesn't. If you keep them neatly arranged in a Library like display, they may not find it when they need.

The teacup with their name tag could be the price won in school for a musical chair. And that could just find a place on the bedside. So, they could look at it every day, and be proud of their achievement.

A holiday picture with Dad, Mom and sister could well be stuck on the wall, just above their bed, with unevenly cut cello tape and colored corners. So, they could look at it every time and Thank God for giving a happy family. If you frame it up and mount it on the wall, it's just another family photograph.

My cleaning missions are well informed ever since, with that sensitivity factor attached. I would rather wait for them to trash them up. Until then, let them enjoy their prized possessions, closer to their hearts, down and under their beds and pillows and right on top of their bedspreads.

VI
Daddisms

The younger one woke me up from a lazy Saturday evening siesta. He was bored with just the handful of Xbox games he had and was exploring the Natgeo channels. mostly looking for anything interesting on the Amazonian rain forests (he can watch the documentaries on the fauna and flora of that echo system for the umpteenth time without flinching an eyelid.)

Partly annoyed by the broken siesta, I was on a vengeance warpath.

"Did your math teacher start any new topic on Friday?"

"Nope. Dad, as you know, we are just revising, because the school year is ending in a few days. Remember, our graduation is on the 5th?"

Yours truly was not ready to give up.

"Hmm, okay. But are you pretty clear on the coordinate system you learned last week?"

Glued on to the screen, where the huge reptile (anaconda) was slithering downstream from a marshy mangrove, he paid no attention to my gradually evolving sermons.

"Listen, I have told you several times to respond instantly when I ask you something. Are you clear on all the concepts related to the coordinate system? Remember that's very important for your geometry basics."

"Dad, we did all of those sums together, we did a test in class, and you signed my score card for that, wasn't it an A?"

Hmmm. Yes.

"Oh, maybe I forgot. But anyway, let's do a few word sums related to the same topic. I am sure it will instill the concepts in you very clearly."

Visibly annoyed, he switched off the television and turned back.

"Dad, how many times did your mom ask you to study when you were in 5th grade?"

Hmmm again, to be honest, never.

"Oh ok, then why are you pestering me with my studies, almost spoiling my relaxed holiday weekend?"

"Well, I just want to make sure you are clear on all the topics and are getting ramped up for higher classes and for those complex topics."

"Dad, did you learn all those complex topics in higher classes with someone following up so closely?"

"Oh. But I was self-disciplined and had the focus."

Another doze of boring daddism from yours truly, mainly to cover up myself.

He went back to the Natgeo channel, the anaconda was now missing from the scene, a multihued tarantula taking the spot instead.

I went back to the reverie.

"Dad, you know what? If you can have the luxury of a lazy Saturday evening, why can't I? Fair enough?"

The age old daddisms don't work anymore, I was apparently annoyed and helpless.

VII

Harry Potter Series

I have never been a fan of the legendary HPS series anyway, until I gathered all my wits to get onto the first in the series, The Philosopher's Stone. And this effort came after being through with severe familial pressures, and sheer isolation of being stupid and ignorant in the small world of HP fans, our home. The mom, daughter and the little one are big time into HP and anything that remotely connects with this superhero. The moment they break into a conversation on HPS, I keep my mouth shut with that blissful ignorance embracing me. I was brazen enough to hold onto my strong argument until recently; that HPS is beyond me, and crossing forty and more grey cells would definitely mean withdrawing to my own usual favorites - Robin Sharma, Alvin Toffler, and the Chicken Soup for the Soul series.

Mom and daughter and the little one stepped onto the Harry Potter store off Wilshire Blvd last Saturday with yours truly accompanying, wearing my arrogant stay away from HPS attitude. While they pondered over the Wizards' cloaks, talking about that special game on broom and balls on air, of costumes of Hagrid and the Professors at

Hogwarts. The little one ran into a poster that said Platform No - 9 3/4, with his sister chasing him up, with mom on their heels. The three of them picked up one each to decorate their bedrooms. Yours truly stood open mouthed, clueless, feeling totally incongruous - a feeling close to being illiterate!

A week later, I am almost through with the first in the series, and here is my initial take:

HPS is legendary and I appreciate the high that the fans get every time a new book hits the stands. It's an altogether new world; with unique characters with their own idiosyncrasies, a strange wizardly world with equally strange paraphernalia. JKR is an amazing storyteller, and her imagination is boundless to say the least, and crystal clear to stay embossed in your minds. The characters, their costumes, mannerisms, the events that unfold are all tough to comprehend unless you go through that emotional reading experience. It's an all-new genre' of literature. Period.

Veering off from my regular reading repertoire, here is one more to do, the Harry Potter series.

VIII

Deeds of Love, Tears of Joy

Driving through downtown LA last evening, I was trying to imagine the city 20years ago. The roads and sidewalks would have been less crowded for sure, with fewer number of upmarket retail chains. I would still imagine that the festive spirits were no different; with X 'mas shoppers sprawling Sears, Macy's, and Kohl's. The renowned bakery in the far east corner would have arrays of X'mas cakes, pies and tarts displayed for its regular clientele and the seasonal shoppers. Not sure if the fancy Spanish eatery and the Mexican Grill were still there in the busy west entrance of Macy's. The public park off the busy roads would have been a hot spot for family crowd, children out to play a game of soccer and lovers looking for a serene and silent place offering the privacy they need. Mo Chika opened their signature restaurant only recently, lest it should have been another favorite for the formal diners.

The starry-eyed little girl walked hurriedly past Leo McComb and his dad (name is just out of my imagination), holding hands with her mom and her little brother. Not sure if they would ever catch up with the mom at all, with her quick steps and determined facial expressions. Her handbag was kind of let loose, made of worn-out clothing with grey kittens painted all over. A tiny half full milk bottle was slightly popping out. The starry eyed was still talking about her dream X 'mas tree, so tall that she would need a stepper to tie up balloons and Santa's hats on top. So thick that she would need numerous stars and lights to cover it up end to end. The mom walked past the biggest shopping outlet, with the little girls right on her toes. The huge Xmas tree on the glass door entrance was decorated with gold and silver stars, with every decor that the starry eyed could think of. Gift socks were tied up here and there, red, and green with white fluffy openings. The lights reminded her of a starry night, the long tailed one on top was kind of dazzling in the gentle breeze wafting through the half open windowpane on the other side.

The girl pulled her mom out to the corner of the sidewalk, and murmured "Mom, can we just have a look at the Xmas trees on sale here? I know we would not buy any of those. I just want to have a look. And if my sister cries for any reason, we can just get out in a jiffy." Mom nodded and the three walked in. The girl walked past the flashy party outfits on display, and the jewelry section. There they were, closer to the wall, with glass doors on the other three sides. The seven feet tall guy on the front row was almost touching the ceiling, and the much smaller one on the other corner was almost waist length to her mom. It was complete with all the decors she wanted. The stars, the balloons, Santa in red velvets and numerous gift boxes were right there, the way she wanted all of them to fall and fit together, giving the tree a pretty dazzling look! Moving closer to the tree, she just shouted out "Mom this is exactly what I want. And you know what, all the decors are right there. We don't need to look for anything else, it's a complete tree. I love it." Mom moved closer too and scanned the price tag.

The girl followed her mom out through the exit, doleful and misty eyed. She knew her mom couldn't afford the tree, but the mere thought of waiting one year even to dream of another was painful. She closed her eyes, and thanked Santa; at least now she knew what she wanted, and how her first X'mas tree should look like. Turning past the corner of the shop, she looked back one last time. Her favorite tree was not there. Someone might have picked it up already, she thought. "It's okay, I can wait. Santa will always keep our wishes in his heart, and he never promises anything but just delivers when the time comes." She ran down the pavement to catch up with Mom and her little sister.

Little Leo McComb came running, holding the Xmas tree with all its decor, balloons and the tiny gift socks dangling all around. Sitting in his car, his dad watched, clicking away a few pictures now and then. The girl, still dreamy and misty eyed, paused for a moment. The mom and her little sister held off to the sidewalk. Little McComb handed over the Xmas tree to the girl and ran off. His shrilling voice echoed all over the busy pavement. "Hey it's okay. I can wait for next Christmas and let this be yours"

Sitting in the Cafe Corner, Mr. McComb narrated this festive incident 20years ago. The starry-eyed girl sat next to him holding their own little one, waiting for the festive season to unfold.

Love is all about those little sacrifices; those remarkable deeds that stand out, and those that unite people!

IX

Hitting Likes and More

I was woken up, pretty much rushed up, by a text message on that lazy Friday evening. It was my cousin living in Long Island. What follows is the particularly amusing conversation we have had over the next several minutes.

"Annaa (meaning elder brother) Did you see the family picture that I posted last night on Facebook? You usually are a regular on FB and I was kind of wondering why there was no response from you. I in fact waited almost a day to see what was coming from you. A comment or at least a like?"

"Oh, I came across the picture, and it was good. I showed it to my daughter, and she liked it too. She spoke about the flawless, trendy gowns your girls were wearing. I was trying to please her and go back to my reveries as quick as I could."

"Annaa - But then, why did not you hit a like?"

"Well, it was your family picture, and I loved everything about it. Your husband - my brother-in-law - was looking great, just out from that Hawaiian vacation you had last month,

handsomely refreshed! And the kids were gorgeous too. Looked like you were having dinner at a fine diner somewhere in the Downtown NYC? Maybe, an upmarket Italian joint? The bottom line - on a pretty clear note - is that I liked the picture and was happy to see that you guys were doing great as a family. Does that really matter if I hit like for the picture on FB or not?"

"Annaa, most of our family members -now connected 24*7*365 via FB - liked it. It looks odd if they don't see your 'indifference' to it. And more so when we live in this part of the world. Pash annan did that the moment the picture was up on my wall."

Now I see the point. Pash (my close pal, who is happily settled in Dubai) does that almost instantaneously and likes to hit those harmless likes to almost all of his friends' pictures. After all, it's a happy world you see and Pash believes in making people happy. The number of likes really does matter, and people keep a close tab on it. Now, look who is missing to complete this 360 deg likes on the virtual world? You better be part of this game; the message is clear.

"Annaa - Again, Jan was so romantic in that shot. Didn't you notice? His head was slightly bent towards mine and was almost kissing me. And Piya and Amy were so cute in their birthday gowns. The drops they were wearing were from Alukkas in Dubai on a stopover in our last India visit."

The facts apart, I was trying to come to terms with the characters seemingly unfamiliar to me.

"Who is Jan?"

"Annaa - Jan is my husband (your brother-in-law) Janardhanan, that's how he is known at work and among family (in US) and friends."

"Oh, ok. I get that. And who is Piya and Amy?"

"Annaa - Piya is Priyadarshini, and Amy is Ambili. Don't you remember our family gathering in India when the twins celebrated their 10th birthday?"

True. We were there with family, and the party was a helluva one. The food was awesome, and you folks made sure everything worked out pretty well. The waterfront venue was ideal for the gala anyway. The twins have grown up a bit, and stepping into the fag end of teens, dropping their sweet names somewhere on the way.

"Now I get it. And how do you go by? Is that still Aparna?"

"Annaa - I picked up Aps (Aps Jan) long back."

Again, I get the point. It is nice to see a loving family enjoying dinner on a lazy Friday evening, in an up-market NYC restaurant. But I need to be sensitized enough to notice the subtleties and specifics in the picture, and more over like it explicitly to convey my appreciation point blank.

"I apologize and will do it the moment I log onto FB next. I need to be social media savvy for sure. But be sure to talk more outside of FB. To me, that's 360deg relationship."

X

Summers, the Boss and the Holidays

This post is about vacations and Paid Time Off that give us boundless fun and frolic with loved ones and a quick breather from those day-to-day grinds and occupational hazards. It is also about those arrogant bosses with an attitude to their co-workers going on holidays.

The series of incidents that unfolded on that much awaited Friday when I secretly planned to hit the freeway at 5PM sharp and rock all the way back home, dump the car in the garage, jump onto the taxi, crowded with wife and kids and that countless strapped baggage, and breathe, and breathe again! Heading home for the summers.

Stage 1: Transition meeting with Alice

Me (all excited with a million-dollar smile): "Hey Alice, we have been working so closely ever since we kicked off this project, and I really don't think we need a transition meeting. Remember, we pulled out all those weekly status reports and colorful dashboards (that don't make any sense to me even when I write this post) together? Do we really need to go over all the work done to date and the upcoming tasks for June? After all, you are one of those brilliant multi-taskers (thought a little bit of buttering would help) in our 150+ team. Am sure you would be one of the key contestants for the most valuable team member of the month award for December 2013."

My blabbering continued, and Alice apparently fell for it.

Alice: "Yeah, I get that. I feel pretty comfortable taking your work forward and do not anticipate anything in June. It should be a cake walk for sure when you are away. By the way, don't forget to bring that kathakali thing for me and the diamond cookies (kaju burfi, a popular Indian sweet)."

Me (sigh): "Oh yeah, my wife has already booked those kaju burfis in one of those popular outlets down south. They are in fact made to order you know."

Sigh again. Alice is out of the way!

Stage 2: Transition meeting with Alice and the Boss

By the way, she is not my friend on FB and if there are mutual friends, please refrain from liking or commenting on this post however tempted you are.

The Boss: "All right guys. My expectation is very clear. I want everything to be seamless as if Roy is here every day, I don't care about PTOs or whatever. Alice, is that clear to you? BTW, how did the transition go? Are you comfortable taking over from Roy and delivering flawlessly in the several days to come? Remember, he will be back only in July."

Alice: "Yeah, on hindsight, I don't think I can handle everything. I know Roy was pretty much pressed for time, but I would be comfortable if all those new processes we spoke about last week are documented."

Everyone, including the boss agreed to defer that task until July, to be completed when I am back from the holidays. Looks like my secret dream of hitting the freeway at 5PM and board the flight on time is a remote possibility. Documenting this stuff would take the whole night, and seriously, I am not in for it now. I need my holidays now, and not any later.

The Boss: "That sounds fair, Roy, do you think you could document that in detail and send back to Alice by mid next week?"

Sigh! "Oh yeah, you bet. My holidays are pretty open, and we have not planned anything much other than just chilling out: Alice is going to have it in her Inbox by mid-week for sure."

I was even ready to promise the moon to somehow get out of the office sooner. With promises on, I managed to hit the freeway at 5PM, and boarded the flight on time, leaving my work laptop home in the midst of those chaos. In the middle of those blissful holidays, it was a nagging pain right on top of my mind. There is no way I can pull out that documentation, the bits, and pieces that I can recollect with my middle-aged memory is not enough to stitch even a half page introduction.

But I am bold enough to return from my PTO with that task unaccomplished, brazen to say the least. Who cares when I am having a whale of a time? The boss and significant others in the workplace miss out the roads to the destinations totally, they have dropped their smiles long back, and their 'hi's and "how are you"s sound metallic, coming from an alley miles and miles away. They deliberately miss to say have fun and enjoy your holidays to a colleague traveling home halfway across the globe. You need a breather, and a smile! I can't donate any because they are my prized possessions.

XI

The Sand Bubblers

One two and three. And then countless others followed. I tried to seek an order in that unfolding chaos, struggling to recollect, what do you call a group of those creepy little creatures? A cast of something?

I was catching my breath and pausing for a second to count them as accurate as I can. As darkness engulfed the sands, I lost track. The potential victims darted in and vanished elsewhere, right in front of my eyes. The roaring waves crashed onto the sands again, wetting them in a fierce first kiss! With that came those creepy little monsters again. One two and three. I always lose that bet, because they disappear as rapidly as they come in to those fragile little bubbles of sand.

The kids came running from the far end of the beach. "Dad, did you see more and more of them coming? I want to hold one of them captive, and of course release it later." The younger one shouted.

But I wonder where they go? Do they have homes pre-built that they seek refuge in a split second? The younger one started digging holes on the sand expecting to find at least one of them deep inside, waiting to escape out into the brave new waters again.

A huge cruise liner was docking into the port. A flurry of tourists flocked the grounds in a moment and almost disappeared into the darkness. The young couple sitting a few feet away were lost in a deep embrace, oblivious to the crashing waves and the unfolding chaos.

One two and three again. I watched in awe as another rapid cast of bubblers crashed in and vanished into those unseen bubbles. The little girl from the other family chased down another bubbler and crushed it in her hands. A drop of white blood remained on her tiny little finger. She laughed in ecstasy and ran away, chasing the next victim. "You are a murderer!" screamed her brother.

For the bubblers, being home is an ephemeral feeling of joy that lasts only till the next monster waves. Life, despair, misery, and an imminent death cast an eternal shadow. And they always bleed in white. Who has blood on their fingers?

PS: Sand bubblers are the little crabs you on beaches. They are cute, aren't they?

XII
The First Flight

My meticulously drafted notes on everything you need to know on your first solo travel rested gloomily in her fancy carry on. The dad's non-stop sermons continued all through the drive to the LAX Airport.

"Though you have done it umpteenth times with mom and dad, let's go over it again - how to get a boarding pass from the kiosk and whom to seek assistance if that doesn't work! How not to express your anxiety and be stunningly confident while seeking help! How the security clearance processes have changed over the years and being attentive to your personal belongings and grabbing them right back post clearance. Figuring out your boarding gate, using your debit card to buy a quick bite from the snack bar and tip appropriately (don't go over, to be sure!). Being attentive to everything the lady at the boarding gate announces, and never take a long toilet break!"

Glancing up from her iPhone, she gave me a quick nod and drifted back into the rapid texting mode with her friends as always. "Dad, I got all that. Now, you trying to scare the hell out of me, whatever it takes?" It was better to focus on my driving than to get caught up on my parental anxieties. She got all that, and I can see the printed cheat sheet popping up from her bag. Relax dad!

Wishing her a safe journey, I stayed there for a while lost in thoughts. She hurried up the escalator, waved back and disappeared into the crowd. Look at that, was she not worried? Would not she miss home, dad, mom and the little bro?

Beep! Her WhatsApp message popped up; "Dad, I am at the gate. The flight is delayed by an hour and a half. See you dad!"

"Hey – wait a sec. The flight is delayed?" I began typing furiously; "go back and read the section on 'what if your flight gets delayed?' section in the cheat sheet."

Like an eagle high up on the sky looking for its vulnerable prey down somewhere, I continued to stare at my screen, waiting for a response.

Beep! "Dad, accidentally, I just tossed that cheat sheet up in the trash. Talk to you soon!"

Well, did it not slip my mind to remind her about the meeting point upon landing? Baltimore is a busy airport and finding the international baggage claims area could be tricky. Didn't want to rely on WhatsApp now; what if she didn't see my message on time? Speed dial #2 *daughter*: "hey this is Deva, am not available at the moment, will call you back as early as I can!" Slowly, I headed back to the parking lot staring at the flight tracker occasionally to see the status changing to 'departed'.

Kids are growing up fast, and soon there will be an empty nest. Won't that come with a feeling of pride as well? You bet!

XIII

Is Santa Real?

Christmas has always been special in our family. And ever since we became a complete one, with our little ones arriving, it became all the more exciting. The Christmas eve shopping, getting the X'mas tree all decked up, wrapping up gifts for the little ones, placing them down under the tree well past mid-night (we need to wait for them to go to bed to do that secret ordeal!). The kids go back to bed, with huge expectations on gifts from Santa.

But then they would also be a wee bit worried, and concerned of not landing up with their much desired gifts, just because they have not been so good the past year, the way Santa wanted them to be. But we would pacify them assuring that Santa would love to see kids the way they are, naughty and sweet; and it's okay to be naughty, without crossing the borders set by Dad and Mom. Both would nod in agreement, and go back to bed, reminding me to set the alarm for 6AM on the Christmas day morning.

Dad and mom would get up well before six, and would be in the kitchen preparing X'mas lunch, and baking the kids' favorite butter cake. The younger one would come in first, rubbing his eyes, walking slowly to the tree, eyes sparkling with expectations, and anxiety. He would kneel down beside the tree and look for the neatly wrapped gift with his name written on it. (To Nandu with all the love, Santa. You 've been a sweet, nice boy the past year. And I love you so much.). It's just too gratifying to see that happiness on his face on receiving his much awaited gift throughout the year. With a big thanks to Santa, he would be back to bed, clinging his favorite gift close to his heart!

The elder one would do exactly the same, as if they have rehearsed the scenes together for a School day play; the expectations, the anxiety and the sweet smile, and the final thanks to Santa.

Well, there has been a twist this year. Everything remained the same, except the realization that dawned on me that my little girl has grown up a bit, and has started thinking logically. The familiar *Star Bazzar* logo on the wrapper made her think twice.

Questions..

"Dad, does Santa know where Star Bazzar is and that's the place where we get big deals?"

"Of course, sweetie. he knows each nook and corner in this world."

""Dad, but then.. shall I ask you a question?"

"Why not? I love you more when you ask questions. Go, shoot."

"Dad, I might be wrong. But on the back of my mind, I have a feeling that you shop these gifts for us. Would you tell me the truth?"

Dad was silent for a moment, debating whether to tell her the truth, and spoil the fun from now on. She would realize that there is no Santa, and dad and mom were acting Santa and playing around. But on the other side, I was happy that my little girl has grown up to figure out stuff.

"Well. dear, you are right. But don't tell Nandu that we are playing Santa for you okay? I want him to enjoy the privilege of ignorance, until he is able to figure out on his own. Do you understand?"

She nodded in agreement. A few moments later. "Dad, it's okay. I promise you. But then does Mama know this truth?"

I just smiled back at her. Another X'mas, and another moment to cherish for a life time.

This is to all the parents around. If you are not playing Santa to your little ones, start from next X'mas. You would enjoy the game, and they too. It would bonus you with a life time of sweet memories.